The Zero Dads Club

Written by Angel Adeyoha

Illustrated by Aubrey Williams

"But it's not all the other kids' fault that you and me
don't have dads," Kai replied.

"LOTS of kids don't have dads! Not just us!
So they should cancel it so that it's fair. Let's have a protest!"

"Or...." Kai said, thinking fast, "we could just make our own project, while the other kids are doing the Father's Day one."

"We can be, like, like a special club! The Moms Only Club!"

"Yeah!" Akilah wanted to be in a special club.
She had two moms and Kai had one mom, so the
Moms Only Club sounded great!

Kai and Akilah made a plan.

MOMS ONLY CLUB

Miss May said they could do it!
They made the announcement at lunch:

"If you want to be in the first grade Moms Only Club,
come to the blue table and we'll do a special project!"

Ellie came over right away. She was really excited to make a card for her Baba. Which is like a Mom, right? And Matias came over to ask if he could be in the club since he's got an Abuela and a Tia.

"But you don't have a Mama, and this is the Moms Only Club, sorry," said Akilah.

"Well, but I don't have a Dad to make a card for," Matias explained.

"It could be...the Zero Dads Club?" said Ellie.
"Because we ALL have zero dads to make cards for!"
Matias looked excited and the kids all agreed to make it official:
the Zero Dads Club.

There was one more kid who didn't have a Dad, but she was shy and didn't come to the blue table.

Kai went over to the table where Melanie was sitting.

"Did you hear about the club? It's the Zero Dads club now,
and do you want to come be in the club with us?
We're gonna make cards!"

Melanie looked up and nodded.

"Ok everyone! Let's all decide what we're putting on our cards!" Akilah said.

She was getting the craft supplies out of the bin.

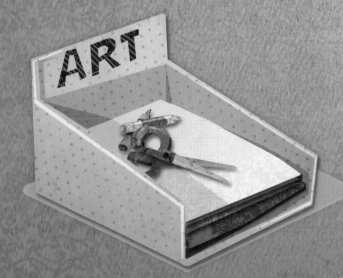

Ellie said, "I think we should take turns and tell about our families so that we can make our cards look like them. We can help each other make them just right."

All the kids really liked this idea. They were so excited it was hard to decide who would go first!

Kai said, "How about Melanie?"
Melanie shook her head and pointed at Kai.

So Kai told about his family....

I live with my mom and my brother. My mom does stuff like shopping for our school clothes and making dinner.

All the kids really liked this idea. They were so excited it was hard to decide who would go first!

Kai said, "How about Melanie?"
Melanie shook her head and pointed at Kai.

So Kai told about his family....

I live with my mom and my brother. My mom does stuff like shopping for our school clothes and making dinner.

But she also does stuff that people say is dad stuff, like playing ball or taking us to the monster truck rally! She's like a mom and dad in one, kinda?

Then Ellie went:

I live with my Mama and my Baba. My Baba is kinda like a girl but kinda like a boy. Baba says she's a butch.

She wears jeans and boots and sometimes ties with her shirts.
She's teaching me how to cook and how to take care of my dog Penny.
She likes to ride her motorcycle and she loves me and Mama!

Then Matias told the kids about his family:

I live with my Abuela and my Tia. My cousins live with us too.
My Abuela has taken good care of me since I was a little baby.

She makes my favorite foods and drives me to school.
My family is so smart we talk in two languages!
We love to watch fútbol and sometimes my Abuela
shouts out GOAL! louder than all of us!

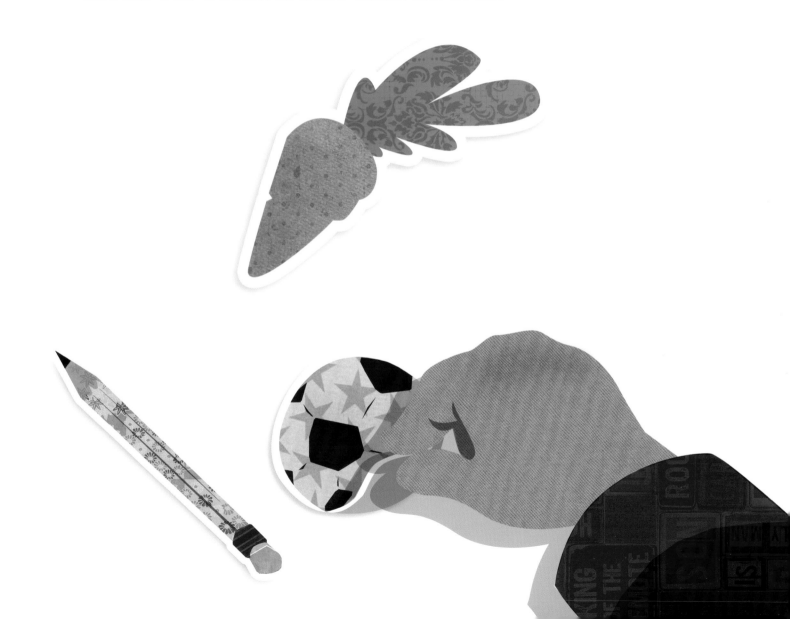

Akilah was next and she was excited! It was hard to be patient and wait!

I live with my Mom and my Mamma. They adopted me when
I was a little baby and my brother and sister too.

Dear Mom & MAMMA,

I want to make my card for them both since they are both like Moms and like Dads. They build things with us and I even got to do the hammer when we made shelves! And they read lots of books with us. I love having a Mom and a Mamma. It's the best!

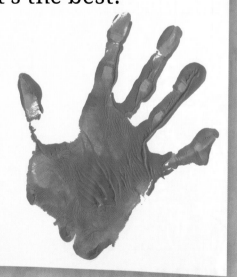

Melanie wasn't sure about talking to all these kids at once.
But everyone encouraged her and she bravely told them her story:

I live with my Ma. We go swimming together and to the zoo.
One day I want to work at a zoo and my Ma says that's a great idea
because animals like quiet and I'm good at being quiet.

My Ma is a really good Ma and I don't hardly miss when she was
my Papa because she's really the same person even though she's my Ma now.

The kids were all so excited to bring their cards home and give them
to their Moms and Mammas, their Babas and Abuelas and Mas.
But they were maybe even more excited about their new club of friends!